PET SHOP HEROES

Story by Stanford Crow

Pictures by Christian Paniagua

BLISS GROUP BOOKS

First published by BLISS GROUP BOOKS™, a division of
BLISS GROUP INC. 725 River Road, No. 32-215, Edgewater, NJ 07020.

Bliss Group Books is the global publishing imprint of Bliss Group Inc. and has companies and representatives throughout the world.

Bliss Group Books is a trademark of Bliss Group Inc. in the United States, the United Kingdom, Europe and other countries throughout the world.

ISBN: 978-1-940021-11-9 paperback

Library of Congress Control #: 2015951371

Text design by Newgen Imaging Systems.

First Bliss Group Books edition: November 2015

2% of the profits of this book will be donated to Kiva.

1. MOSQUITO MADNESS

In a small pet shop on a street near you live four animals who must never be adopted. And that's OK for now. Grace the guinea pig, Carmine the chameleon, Petruchio the puppy, and Kitty the cat have something else to do.

They save the world!

***

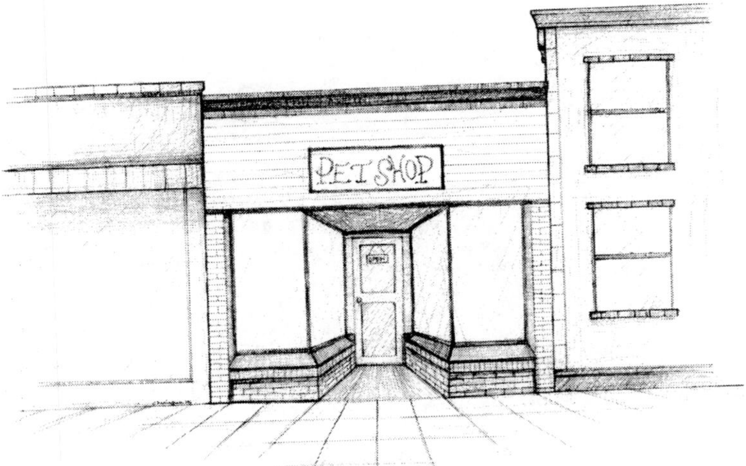
PET SHOP

A few weeks ago, while the world slept, an evil snake called Sly was making a magic potion in his secret laboratory under a garage near you.

He planned to use the magic potion to take over the world.

But just as he was about to finish it, something went wrong.

KA-SIZZLE!

CRASH!

BOOM!

The snake's laboratory exploded!

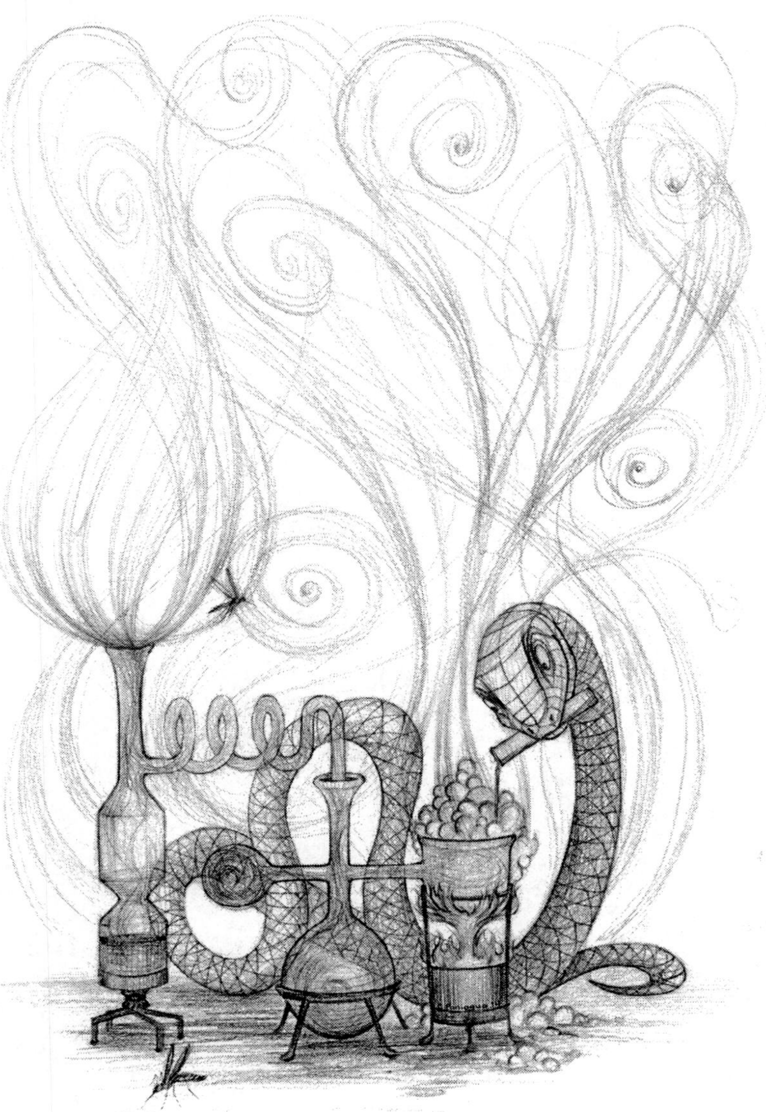

His potion turned into a gas, and the gas floated away!

Sly the snake slithered after the gas as fast he could.

The gas drifted toward a pond.

A Mosquito flew through the gas.

A Fish jumped and swallowed the Mosquito.

And then the Fish started to fly!

Aha! Sly thought. *The Mosquito flew through the gas.*

The Fish ate the Mosquito.

Now the Fish can fly.

The Mosquito's bites are magic because my gas is *magic!*

The flying Fish coughed.

The Mosquito fell out of the Fish's mouth and landed on Sly.

Sly smiled at the Mosquito and hissed, "Bite me."

"What?" asked the Mosquito, who was having a very weird day.

"Bite me!" Sly said.

"No problem!" The Mosquito bit the snake.

Sly laughed an evil laugh.

"MWA-HA-HAAA!

"Now I have a superpower! I will take over the city, and then . . . the world!

"MWA-HA-HA-HAA-HA-HA-HA-HAAAAA!"

The Mosquito flew away.

But a little pond turtle called Mud saw the whole thing. She chased after the Mosquito as fast as she could—v-e-r-y s-l-o-w-l-y.

2. HERE'S MUD IN YOUR EYE

At the pet shop near you, Kitty the cat awoke from her morning nap.

She stretched as usual.

She yawned as usual.

But when she jumped at a fly, something *un*usual happened.

Kitty did a triple flip with a twist and landed with the fly caught in her claws.

"*Purrr*plexing," she purred happily.

"I have new acrobatic skills. *Marrr*velous, yet strange."

She let go of the fly and jumped out of her cage with a double flip and a cartwheel.

Kitty opened the locks on the cages of her friends—Carmine the chameleon, Grace the guinea pig, and Petruchio the puppy.

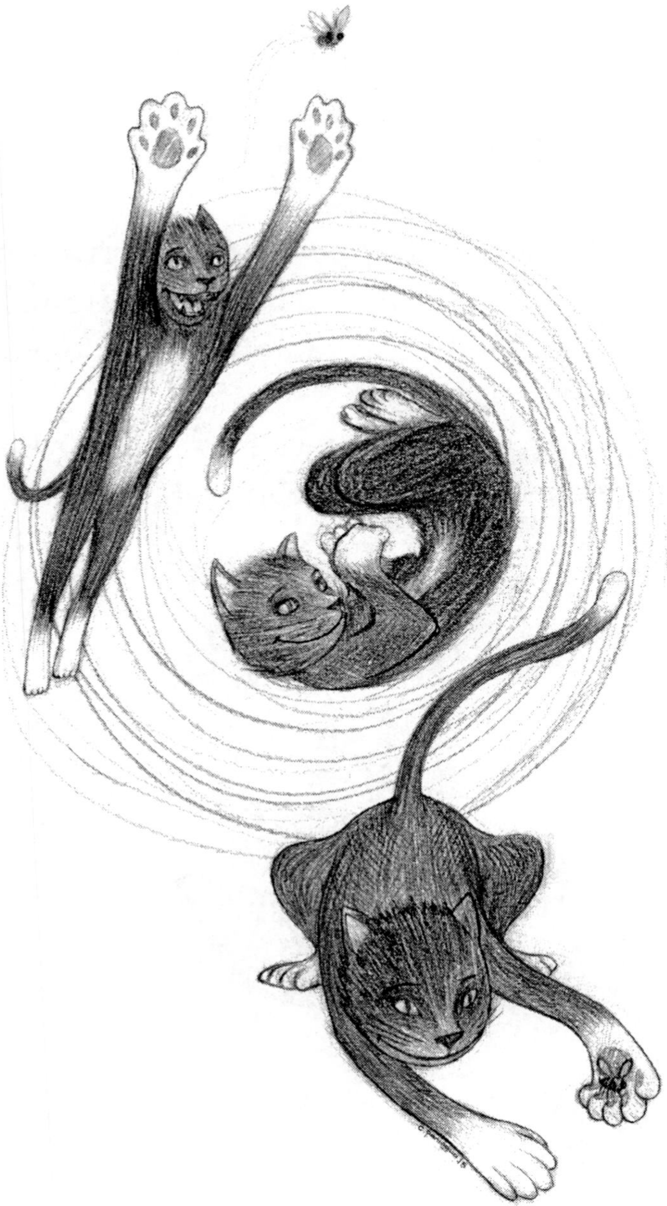

Carmine jumped onto a shelf to read a science book.

Grace did an art project.

Petruchio chased his tail.

Just then, the little pond turtle arrived in the pet shop doorway. She had been running all night. She yelled, "Hello! My name is Mud! Help!"

Nobody heard her.

So, when Petruchio raced by chasing his tail, she stretched out her neck and bit him.

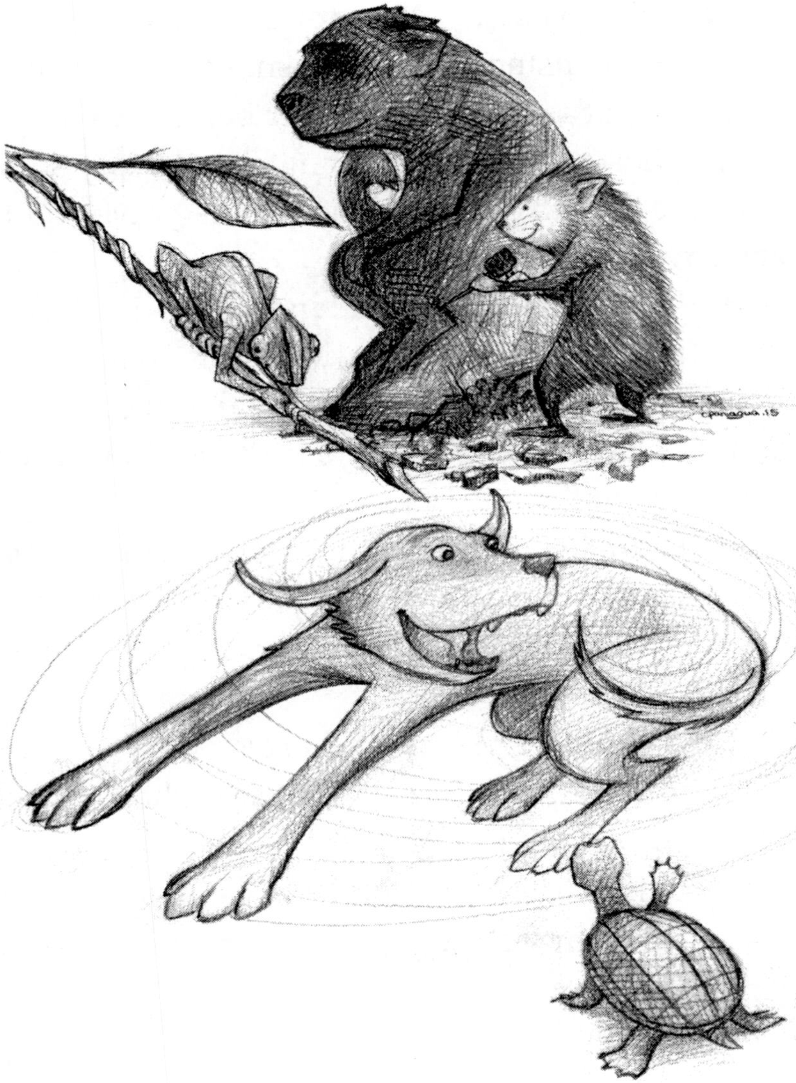

"Ow!" Petruchio shouted, "I got me!"

"No, that was me," Mud said. "I am most sorry indeed. But listen! There's a snake at the pond who just got a superpower after being bitten by a magic Mosquito and he's going into the city so he can take over the world! Only the magic Mosquito can save us. Is she here?"

Kitty did a backflip and landed beside Mud.

Kitty said, "There's no Mosquito here. Slow down and tell me all about it, my *frrr*iend."

Grace muttered, "Telling a turtle to slow down. *That*'s funny."

Kitty looked Mud in the eye (she knew that good leaders always look everyone in the eye) and asked, "What kind of power-*rr* does the snake have?"

Mud shook her head. "I don't know."

"Hmmm," Kitty purred, and scratched herself. "Let's think about this."

Carmine saw Kitty scratch. He also saw Petruchio and Grace scratch. And Carmine had an itch, too.

"A-ha!" Carmine shouted, **"SCIENTIFIC METHOD!**

"(1) **QUESTION!** Has the Mosquito been here?

"(2) **OBSERVATION!** We are all scratching our-selves. We all have mosquito bites.

"(3) **GUESS!** We have all been bitten by the magic Mosquito.

"(4) **TEST!** Do we have any new superpowers?"

Petruchio flapped his ears and suddenly lifted off the ground. He could fly!

Petruchio woofed, "I can gumblebee!" (Like a lot of puppies, Petruchio often gets too excited; and when he gets too excited, he mixes up his words.)

Grace pulled on the bars of a cage. The bars bent and snapped! She laughed. "I got super strength!" She bent the cage bars into the shape of a turtle and gave it to Mud.

Kitty leaped into the air, bounced off the ceil-ing, and landed beside Carmine. "I have become the wo*rrrr*ld's g*rrr*eatest acrobat."

Carmine shouted, "(5) **CONCLUSION!** We have superpowers!"

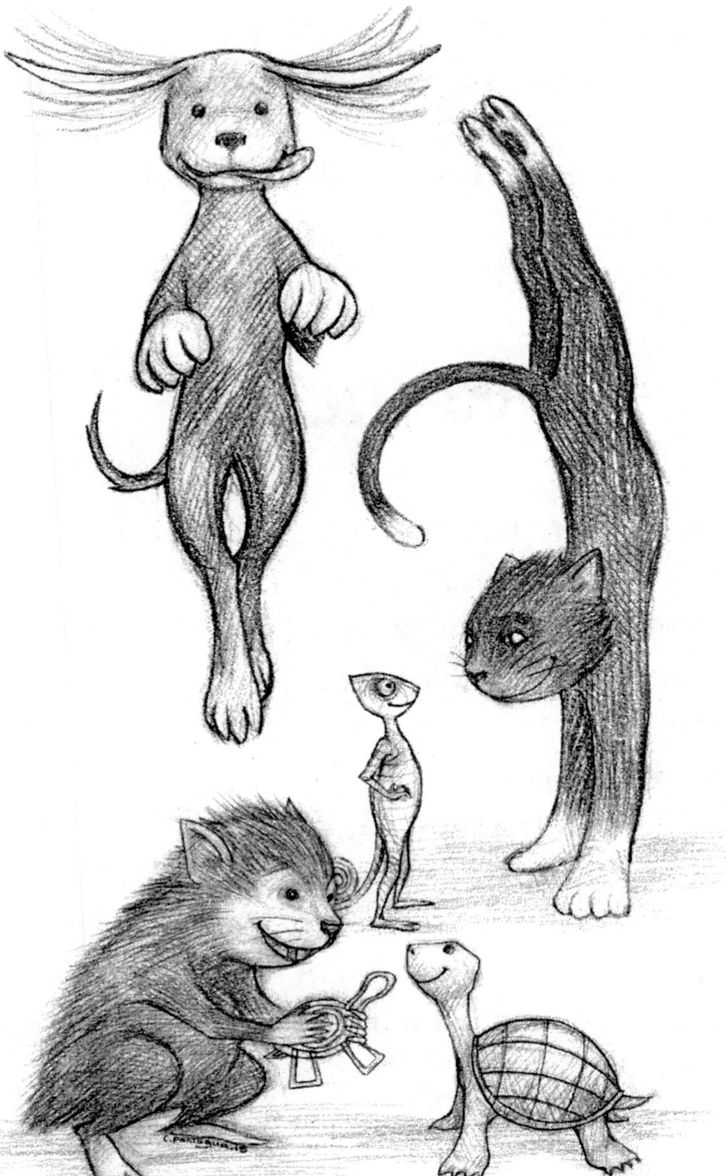

"Friends!" Kitty said, "We must pu*rrr*-sue the greater good! Let's stop the snake! Let's save the world!"

Petruchio barked, "Yeah-yeah-yeah! Let's pave the swirl!"

He flew out the door.

WHOOSH!

And then he flew right back in and asked, "Where's the world?"

Kitty asked the puppy, "Hasn't anyone told you to look before you leap?"

Petruchio stared at her. "Is that a cat thing? Can we just go?"

"Yes!" Kitty purred, and the four animal friends charged out of the store and down the hill toward the pond and the city center beyond.

Mud called after them, "Be careful! That snake is evil! And you don't know what his super-power is!"

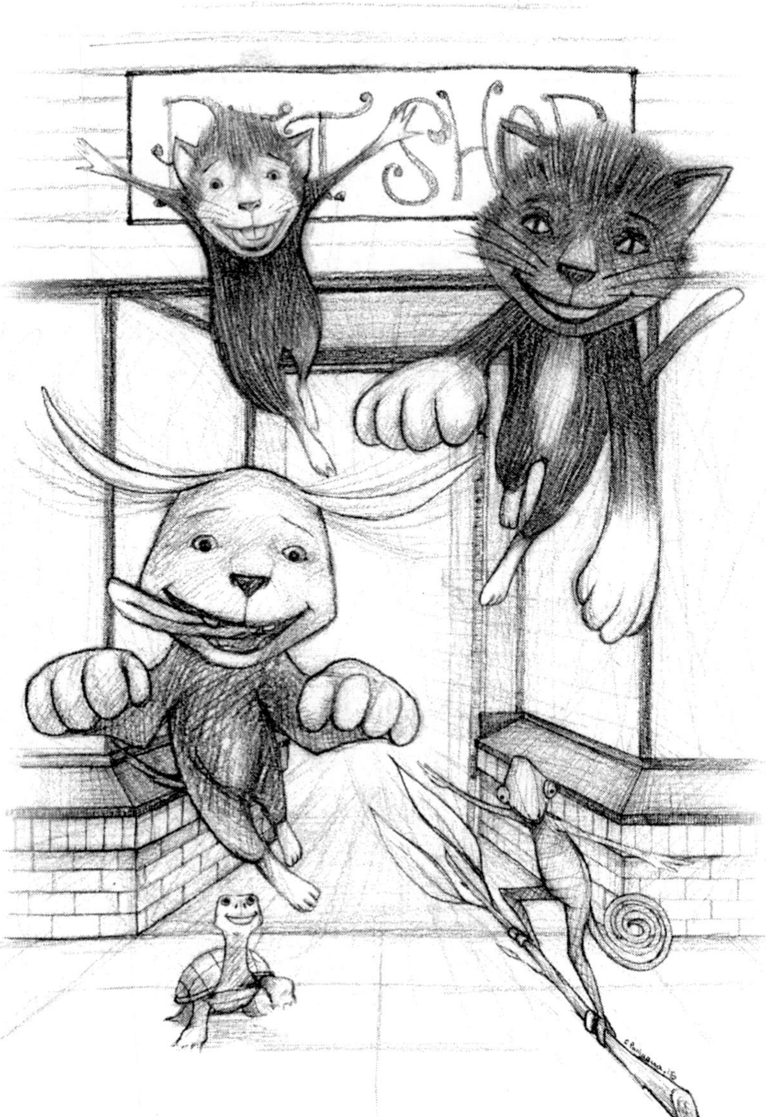

3. Something Wicked This Way Slithers

The Pet Shop Heroes charged into the city.

As they ran past the fire station, Kitty pointed down the street to the Mayor's house. A crowd of people were carrying a snake right up to the Mayor's front door!

The snake shouted, "Madame Mayor! I, Sly, the Great and Magnificent *Ss*-snake, wish to *ss*-speak with you!"

The crowd of people shouted,

"Mayor! *Ss*-speak to the *ss*-snake! *Ss*-speak to the *ss*-snake!"

Grace said, "I think we found the evil snake."

Kitty hissed, "Yes! But why are people helping him?"

Carmine said, "SCIENTIFIC METHOD! (1) QUESTION! What is the snake's power? (2) OBSERVATION! Nice people are doing what the evil snake wants. (3) GUESS! The snake is controlling their minds!

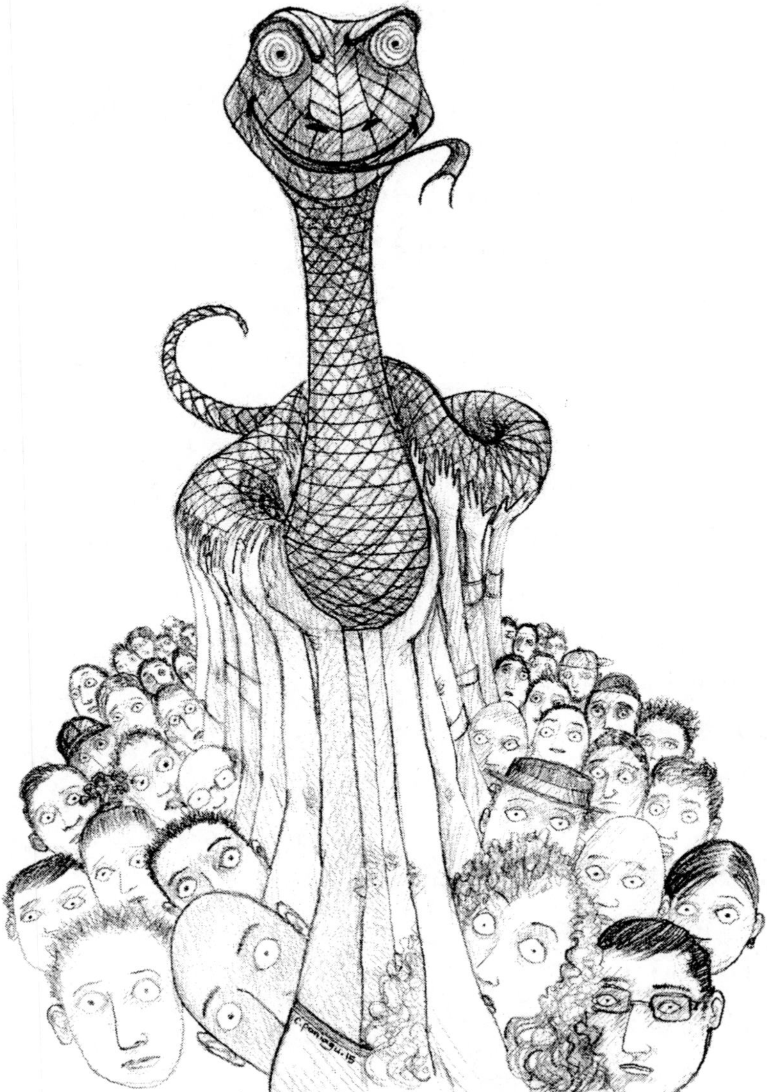

Shocked, Petruchio fell out of the air and said, "Buy a polliwog!"

"What?" Kitty asked. "'Buy a polliwog'? Did you mean to say 'diabolical'?"

Petruchio nodded. "Yeah. Bad! Let's stop him!"

Grace smacked her fists together. "It's bongo time!"

"Wait," Carmine continued. "We need more data! SCIENCE! I'll investigate!"

Grace pointed a furry claw at Carmine. Her whiskers twitched angrily. "Just a flea-picking minute! The puppy flies, Kitty's an acrobat, and I got super strength. What do you got?"

Carmine grinned slyly at her. "Here's something I can do, and I'll do it just for you." He held out a claw and bent his thumb to touch his fingers. Then he changed colors. "Any more questions?"

Grace yelled, "Hold up! You were *born* with opposable thumbs—and you've always been able to change colors. You're a reptile—like the snake. Are you a *spy*?"

Carmine said, "We need more data! I'll be back!" And he used his camouflage to disappear.

Just then the Mayor's front door opened.

The crowd said, **"Speak to the *ss*-snake!"**

A man in a suit looked at Sly and raised his foot to step on him.

Sly said, "Goons! Stop the Stop-us-*ss!*"

Six big men said, "We are the Goons! We will stop the Stop-us-*ss!*" Their eyes glowed red.

They jumped up from the crowd and grabbed the man in the suit, holding him steady while Sly stared into his eyes.

Sly's eyes glowed red.

Now the man in the suit bowed to Sly and said, "Come right in, *ss*-Sir."

Sly slithered inside the Mayor's house. The door closed behind him.

"Let's go!" Petruchio woofed. "We have to mop that cake!"

"Wait!" Grace grabbed him by the tail. "I been thinking. Superheroes always got costumes, right?"

Kitty licked a paw. "*Rr*-right! Costumes. To protect our identities. But we must hurry."

Petruchio woofed, "Right! Protect dentistry!"

4. Can't Stop the Stop-Us

Grace knocked down the door of the Mayor's house with a big punch—

POW!

—and stepped inside.

She was wearing a bright red mask, and she had painted five red Gs on her chest.

The five Gs stood for "Great Grace the Guinea piG, Get out of my way."

Petruchio flew inside doing karate moves. He was wearing a dinosaur hat, a red mask, and a small red cape.

Kitty did a triple backflip. She was wearing a red cat suit with a matching red mask.

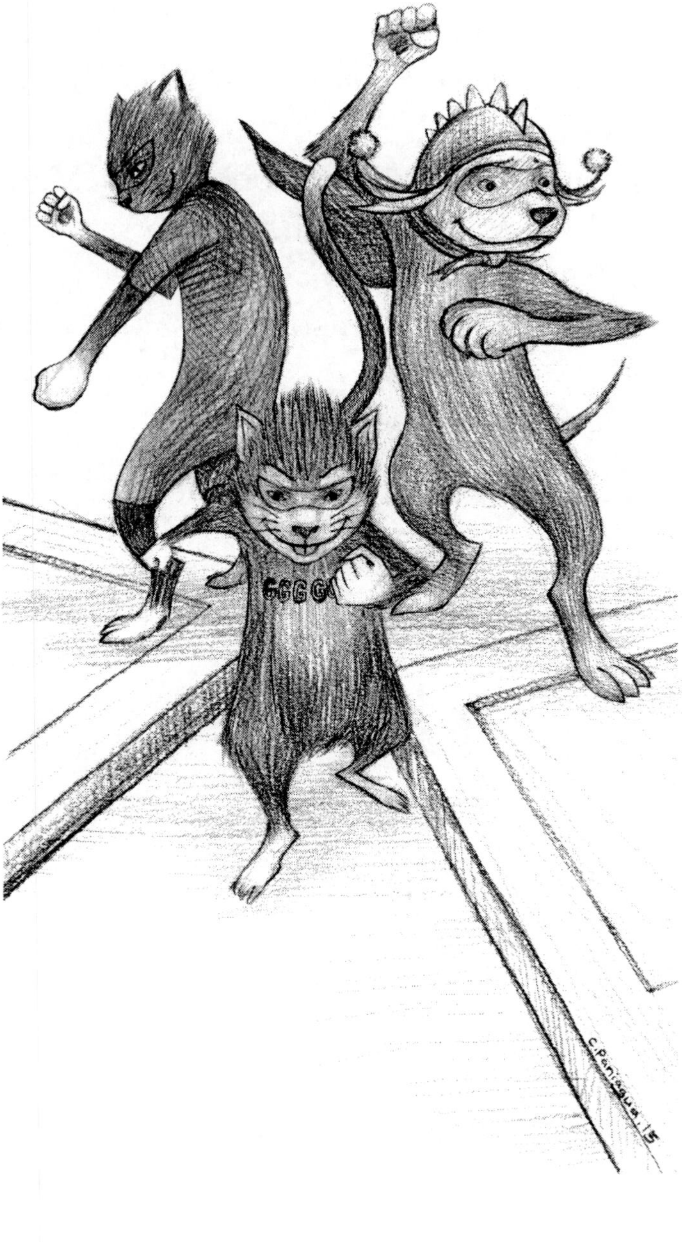

Across the room, two Goons were holding the Mayor while Sly slithered toward her, his eyes glowing **red**.

Kitty meowed loudly, "Look away Madam Mayor-*rrr*! Look away! And have no fear-*rr*, the Pet Shop Heroes are—"

She didn't get to finish. Sly said, "Goons! *Ss*-stop the Stop-us-*ss*!"

The big Goons attacked the Pet Shop Heroes with wastebaskets and books and their fists.

OOF!

BANG!

KA-BOOM!

KA-BOP!

Meanwhile, Sly wrapped his tail around the Mayor's head, forced her to look into his eyes, and

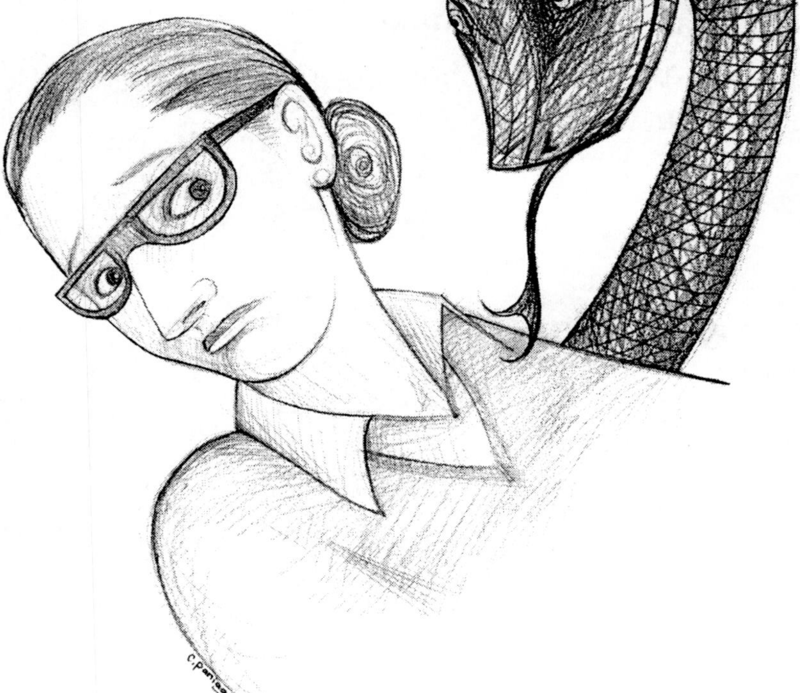
C.Paniagua.15

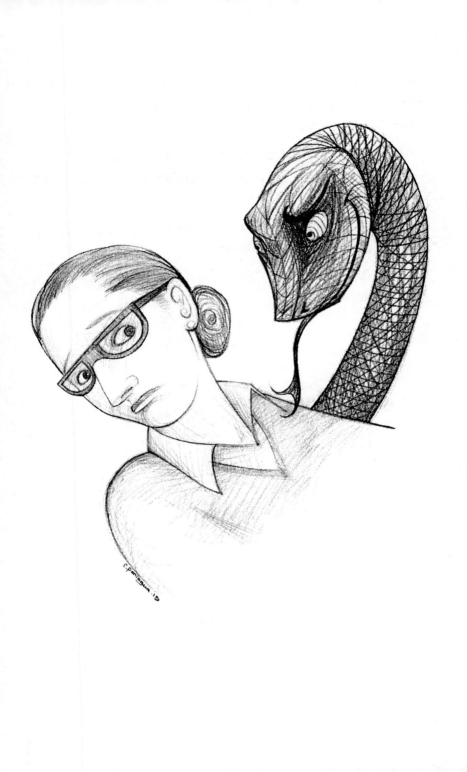

said, "Madame Mayor, do exactly as I *ss*-say. You will help me talk to the President . . . and take over the world!"

Kitty back-flipped away from the Goons. She said, "Petruchio! Stop that snake! Grace and I will keep the Goons busy!"

Petruchio flew as fast as he could toward the evil snake. "I'll mop him!"

Goons swung brooms at the puppy.

Petruchio dodged

← LEFT

and

RIGHT →

and

UP ↑

and

↓ DOWN

He was almost there—

Petruchio opened his mouth to bite the snake when—

—the flying Fish hit Petruchio like a missile.

The blow knocked the puppy all the way into the kitchen and into a bowl of spaghetti.

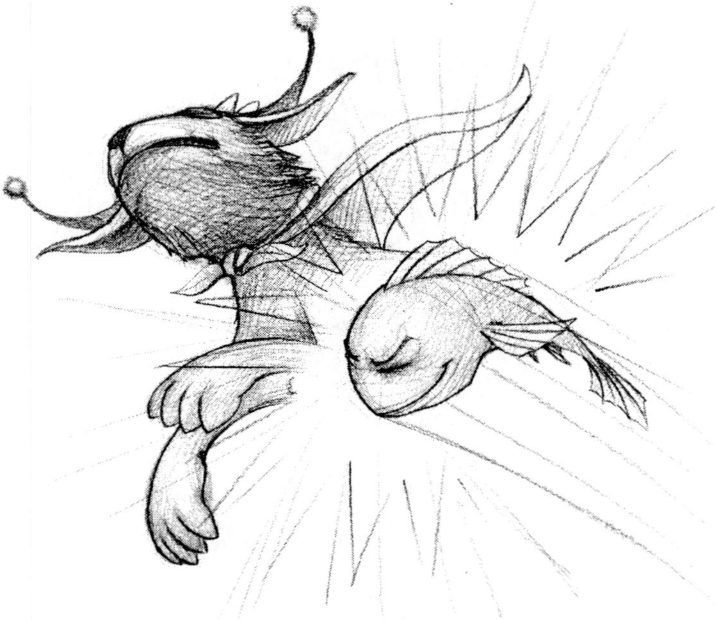

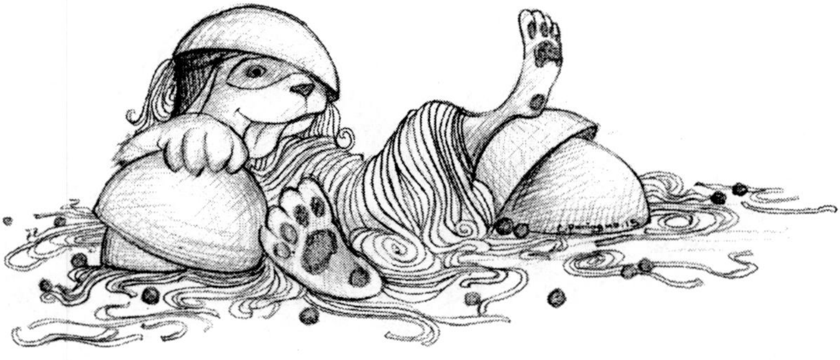

The Fish dropped a lid on Petruchio's head and said, "I stopped the Stop-us-*ss*."

Meanwhile, Kitty and Grace worked as a team.

The Goons dove at Kitty, but she dodged between them and they banged into each other—

BONK!

—and fell to the floor.

Grace bowled them out the door.

SWOOSH!

But the Goons kept coming.

One Goon had a net. He swung it at Grace, but Kitty did a spinning cartwheel with her claws out.

She shredded the net as she went over to her friend's side.

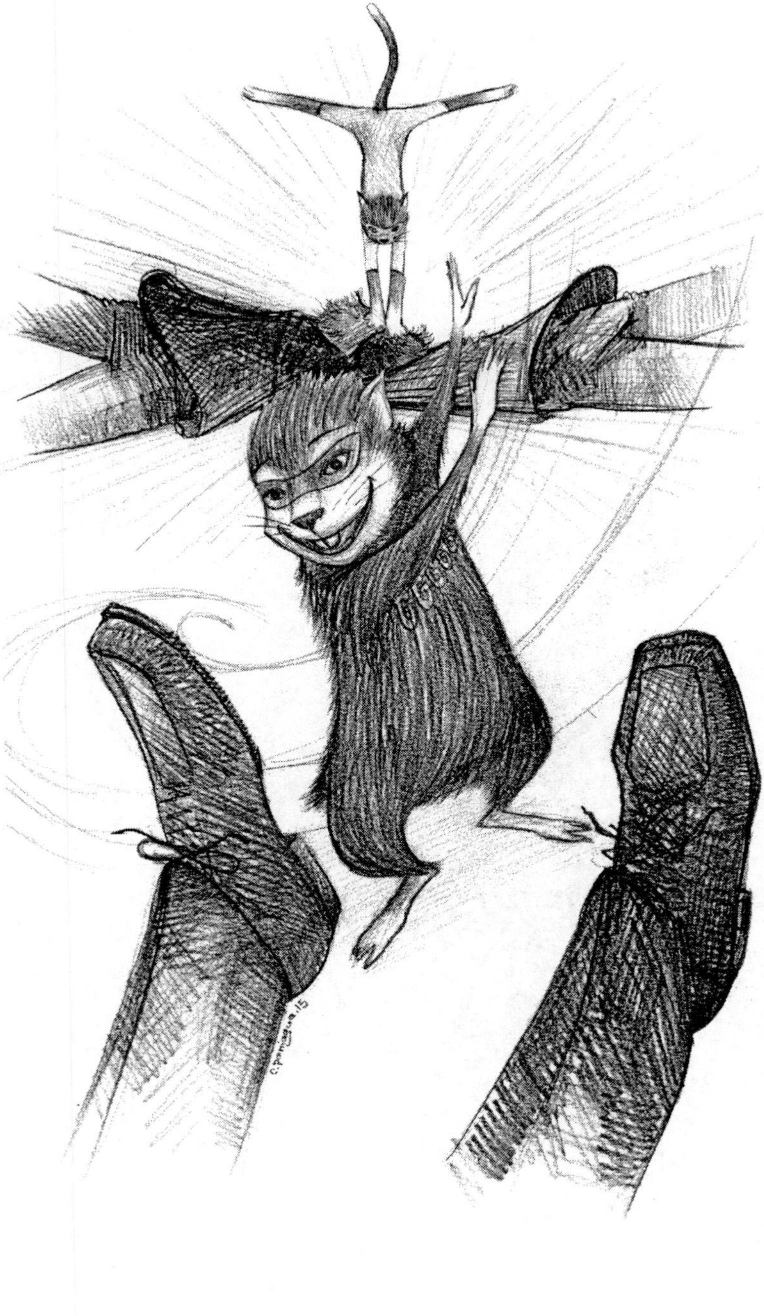

But the Goons just thumped their fists against their chests and attacked again, saying, "Stop the Stop-us-*ss!*"

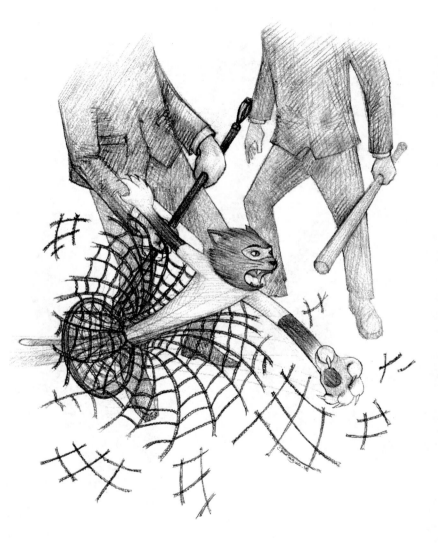

BOFF! WHAP!

And now the Mayor said to the snake, "You are the Great and Wonderful *Ss*-snake; I will do exactly as you *ss*-say. I will call the President and help you take over the world."

The snake said, "Great. Use the computer. I want to look the President in the eyes-*ss*."

5. WHEN THE BAD GET TOUGH, THE GOOD GET SILLY

Back in the kitchen, Petruchio woke up in the bowl of spaghetti. He was stuck, but he still had work to do.

Petruchio chewed his way loose—*GRRR!! YUMM!!*—and zipped back toward the snake, covered in spaghetti sauce and noodles.

The flying Fish attacked again.

But this time Petruchio was ready. He flew faster toward the Fish than the Fish flew toward him.

ZAM!!

The puppy banged into the Fish.

The Fish bounced out of the window.

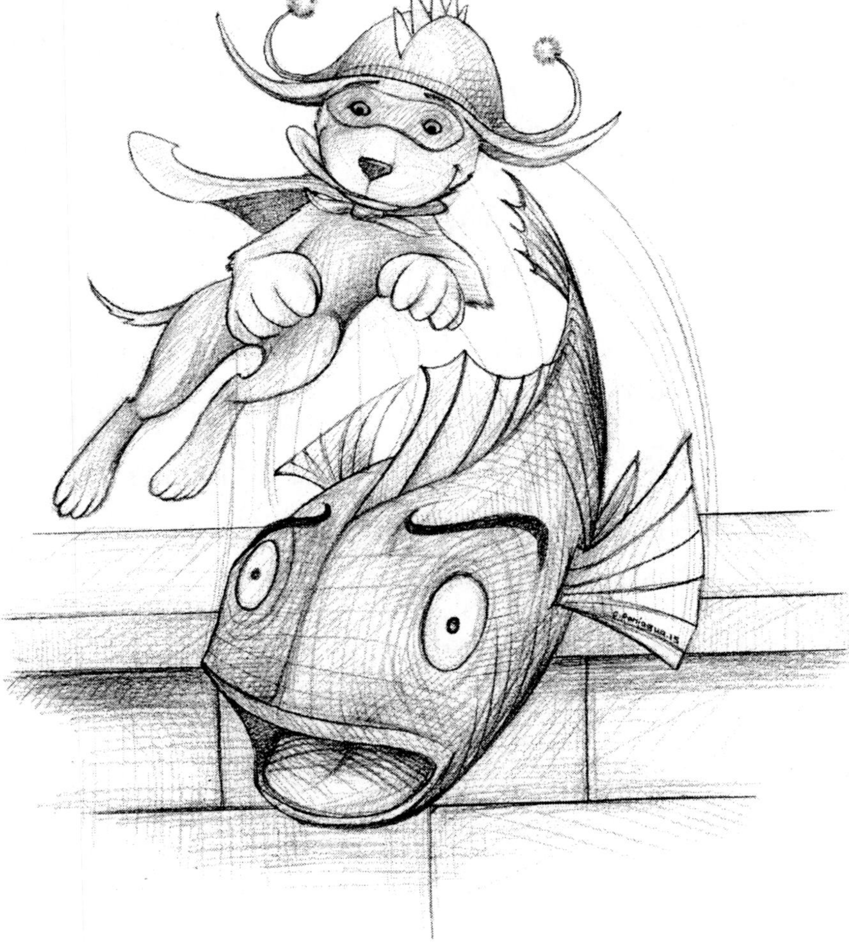

Now, Petruchio flew over Sly the snake and barked—"Cake! That's enough hopscotch outta you! Prepare to meet your potato."

Sly blinked. "What?" he said. "What does that mean?"

And just for a moment, the snake's eyes crossed in confusion.

And as his eyes crossed, just for that moment, something happened.

The Goons stopped attacking.

The flying Fish flew off to look for a river.

The Mayor stopped listening to the snake.

It was just for a moment, but sometimes a moment is all you need.

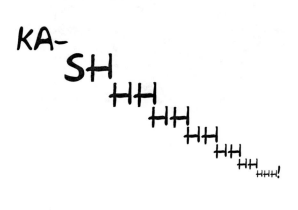

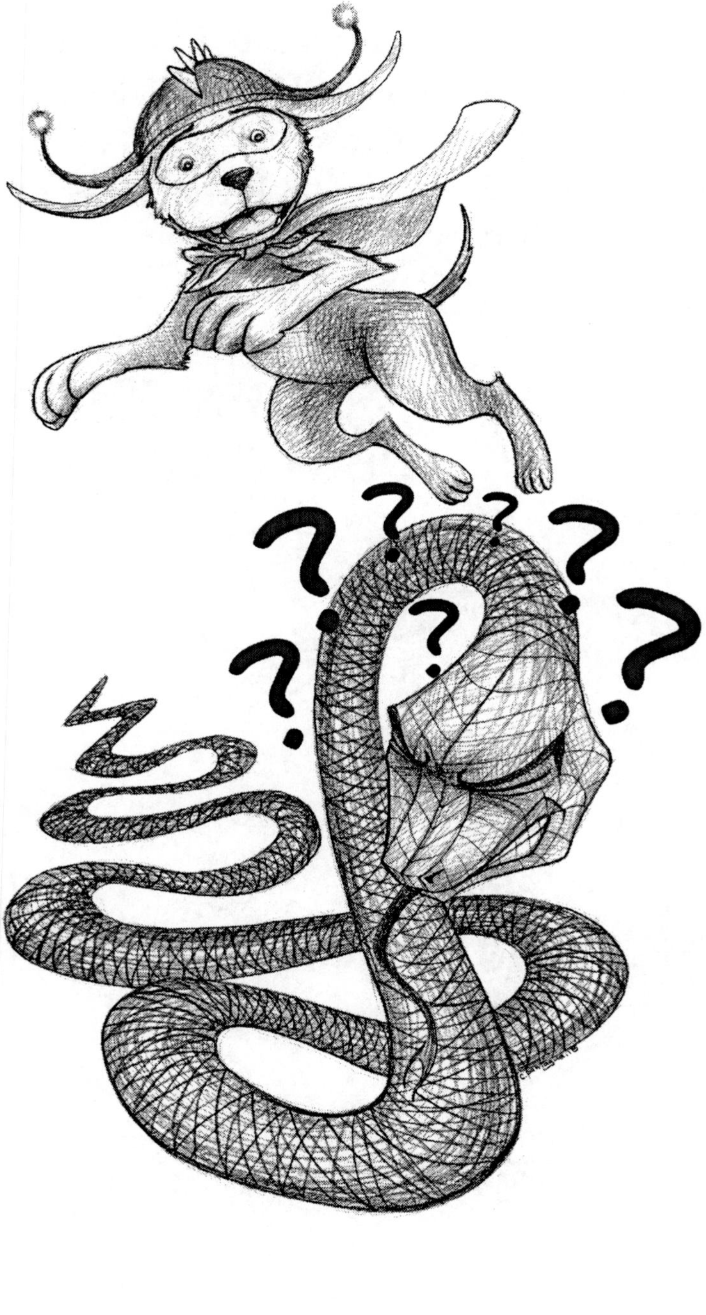

Carmine suddenly reappeared in the middle of the Mayor's living room. He shouted—

"A-ha! SCIENCE! OBSERVATION!"

Grace snarled, "Don't talk to us! You're a spy! You left us when we needed you!!"

SCIENCE!
OBSERVATION!

Carmine said, "I had to observe. We needed more data. And I got it! Just now, the snake was confused, and his mind control stopped. So . . ."

"Yes-*ss*!" Sly interrupted. "My mind control did *ss*-stop. But now it's back. So . . . ," he hissed, "Goons-*ss*! Crush that lizard! Destroy these mammals-*ss*! Mayor—*ss*-sit down and talk to the President."

The Mayor sat down.

The Goons attacked the Pet Shop Heroes.

CLONK!

ZOK!

BONK!

Carmine shouted: "Listen! We can beat him with the SCIENTIFIC METHOD!"

Petruchio barked, "Yeah! But him with terrific breath mints!"

Carmine said,

"(1) QUESTION! How do we stop the snake's mind control?

"(2) OBSERVATION! When the snake is confused, his power can't be used.

"(3) **Guess!** Confuse the snake, and we'll all be saved.

"(4) **Test!** Puppy! Tell the snake your favorite joke!"

Petruchio woofed, "Hey, snake! How many chicken fingers does it take to screw in a light bulb?"

Sly asked, "How many?"

"**Pizza!**" Petruchio yelled.

The puppy fell to the floor and rolled around laughing.

"That doesn't make *ss*-sense," Sly hissed. "It's-*ss* not even a joke—how can you?—don't you realize that—?"

Sly's mind-control power stopped again.

Kitty yelled—"Everyone! Get away! Now!"
The Goons and the Mayor ran away—because no one really wants to help an evil snake.

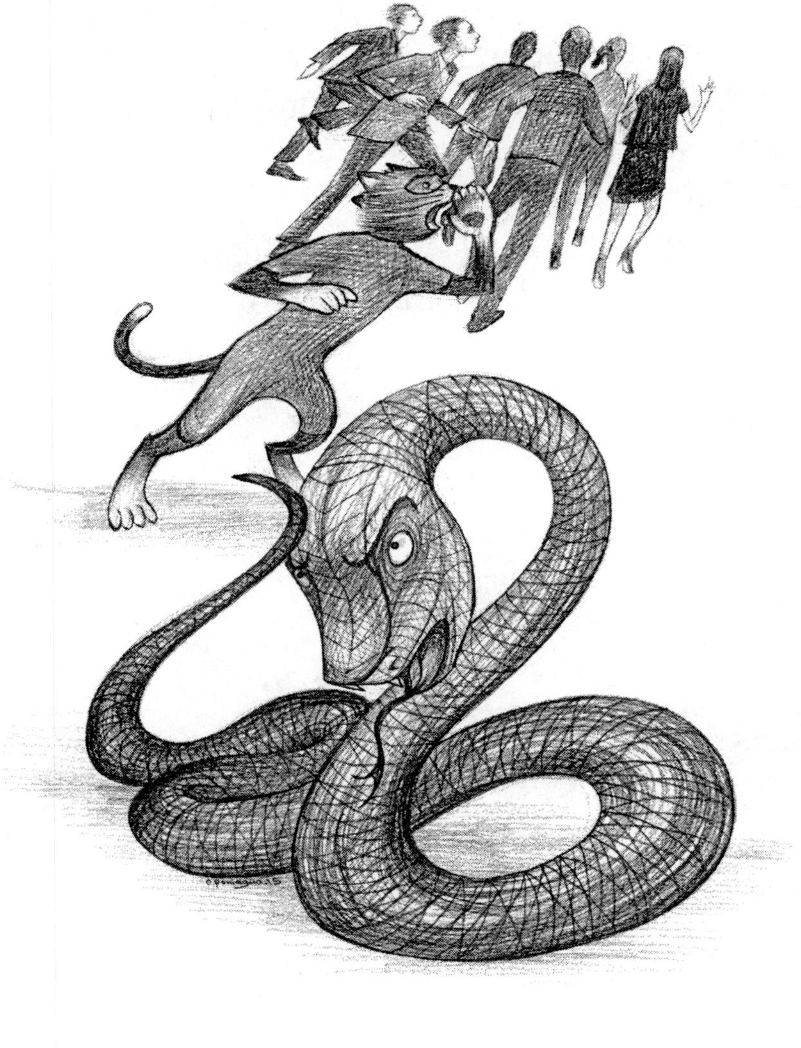

Carmine shouted, "(5) CONCLUSION! Confuse the snake and he has no power! Puppy! Keep talking."

But Petruchio couldn't keep talking.

Because Sly had wrapped his powerful body around the puppy.

Sly hissed, "One *ss*-step closer, and I hurt the puppy!"

Petruchio gasped for air.

Kitty said, "Release him! Ruffian!"

Grace snarled, "You let him go . . . or I'll . . ."

The evil snake hissed, "I, Sly, will let the puppy go . . . after you bring me back the Mayor and she does what I *ss*-say."

Carmine said, "OK, snake. You win. You beat us. You're too smart. And listen, we're both reptiles, we both like science, so . . ."

"I KNEW it!" Grace shouted. "SPY!"

"Excellent," Sly smiled at Carmine. "Join me. We will make a ss-super reptile planet."

"Really?" Carmine said. "I can join you? We'll do science together? That sounds great. Is that a deal?"

Sly nodded. "Of courssse."

Carmine said, "Let's shake on it."

Sly coolly held out his tail to shake.

Carmine took Sly's tail between his claw and thumb.

Carmine's thumb **glowed**.

Carmine's thumb **sparked**.

Carmine's thumb shot off fireworks and smoke.

ZA-ZAP!

ZA-WHOOSH!

When the smoke cleared, the evil snake was gone.

Grace asked, "What in good gravy did you just do to him?"

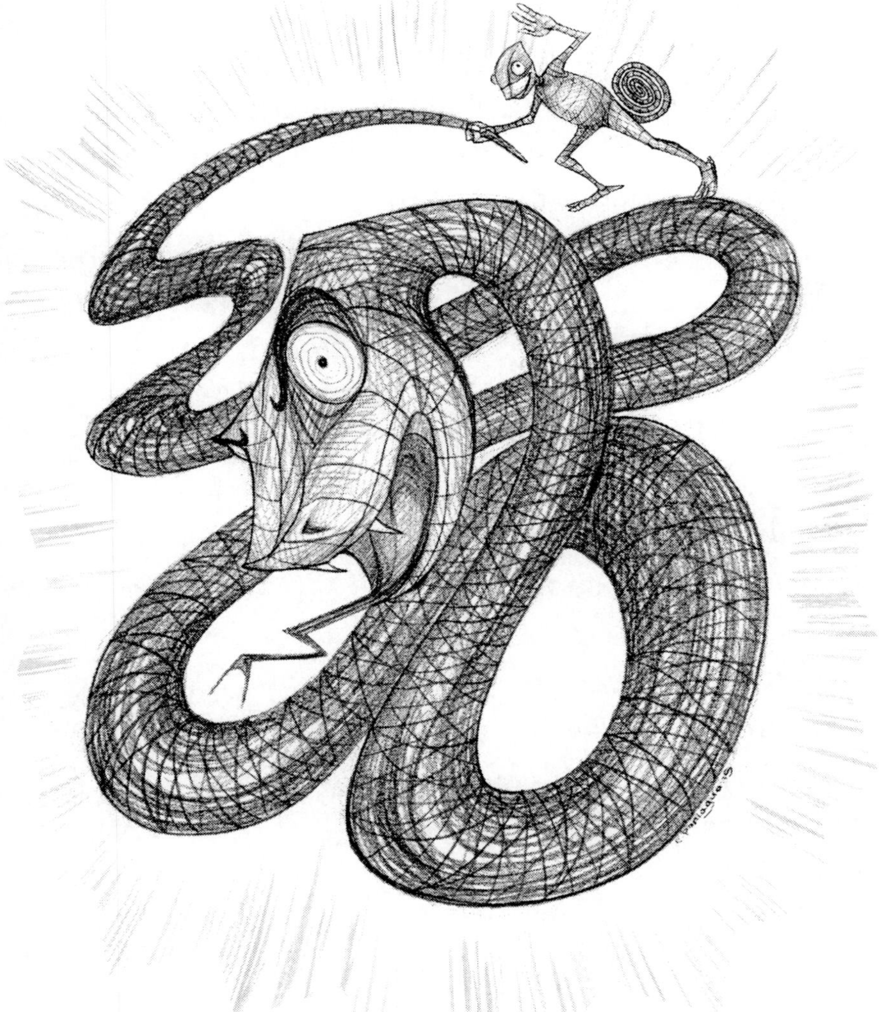

Carmine held up his still-glowing thumb, "Never underestimate the power of the opposable thumb."

Petruchio woofed, "The cake dis-a-peached!"

Carmine nodded, "'Disap*peared*,' Petrucchio. The snake will re-appear in the city jail, where I just transported, or sent, him."

"Trans-poodled! Sent!" woofed Petruchio happily.

"Wow, Carmine," Grace muttered. "We better get you a costume. You're a superhero."

The Mayor walked back into her house with her guards. She looked around the room nervously. "Hello? Everything OK in here now?"

Carmine disappeared so he wouldn't be recognized.

Kitty answered, "Everything's fine now, Madame Mayor-*rr*."

"You're sure?" asked the Mayor. "The whole town was acting crazy. There was that horrible snake."

Kitty looked at her three friends. "Nothing the Pet Shop Heroes can't handle, Madame Mayor."

The town, the nation, and the world were saved.

6. WHEN THE END IS THE BEGINNING . . .

Our heroes went back to the pet shop near you—the perfect hideout. They live there still. Grace made Carmine a red mask, and they all hid their costumes under the food dish of a big dog called Murglerizer.

They all chose Kitty to be their leader.

Petruchio tried to make up a Pet Shop Hero Oath: "All for fur, and fur for all, except uh, for— the rep-linoleum, which—"

"Rep*tile*, Petruchio."

"Yeah! No fur! So..."

"Let's just shake on it and work on our oath later."

"OK!"

Now, if someone comes into the pet shop near you and tries to adopt one of the Pet Shop Heroes, they pretend to be sick or uninterested.

The Pet Shop Heroes wait, they plan, they grow stronger—knowing that at any moment they may be called upon once again to pave the swirl—er, save the world.

And they'll be ready.

THE BEGINNING IS THE END.

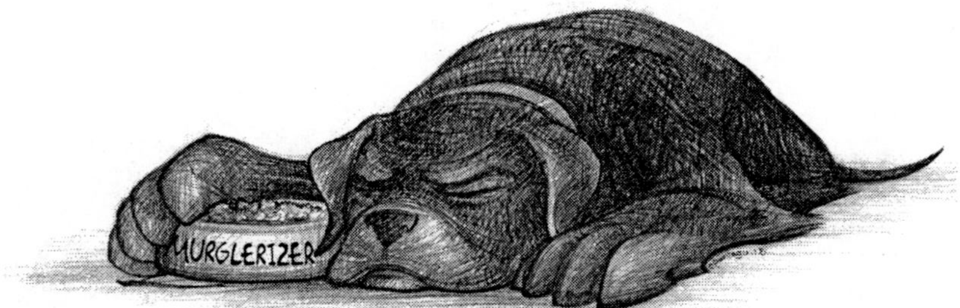
MURGLERIZER

CPSIA information can be obtained
at www.ICGtesting.com
Printed in the USA
FFOW01n0400261015
18015FF